AMANDA'S BUTTERFLY

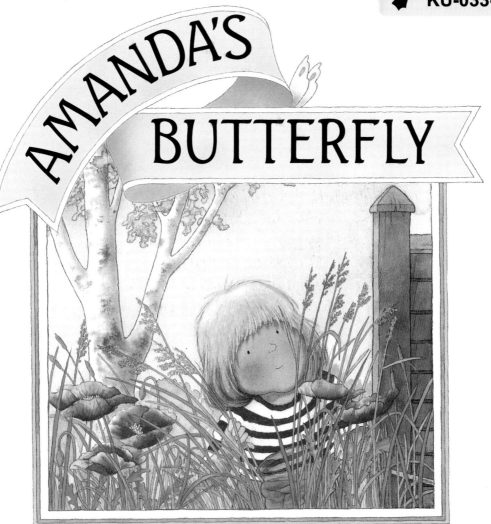

NICK BUTTERWORTH

CARNIVAL

One sunny morning,
I woke up before anybody else
in the house. I sat up in bed and
read a story to my friends...

It was a story about a butterfly.

The story gave me an idea. I decided to catch a butterfly. All I needed was . . .

My butterfly net!

Out in the garden, I looked for a butterfly amongst the flowers. You have to move slowly with butterflies. They hide if you're too twitchy.

I think I must have twitched by the chrysanthemums. I decided to look in a patch of long grass and poppies at the end of the garden.

Suddenly the sun went in. The sky filled
with clouds. Then it started to rain.

The rain got heavier. I thought I'd better take shelter.

I sat in the shed and waited. I watched the
rain splashing on the windowsill and in the
puddles on the path. It went on and on.

Suddenly, a little box of screws fell onto
the bench next to me. It made me jump.
What made it fall?

Then I knew! Behind the box I could just
see the tip of a beautiful wing.

Very slowly, I reached out for my butterfly net.

But as I pulled away the box . . .

I got a big surprise! It wasn't a butterfly.
It was a fairy! A real fairy. A really real fairy!

The fairy looked upset.

She had torn her wing on some thorns.
She couldn't fly and because she couldn't fly,
she couldn't get back home.

I knew I must help the fairy, but I didn't know how. I told her not to worry.

My Dad's good at mending things.
He nailed the door back on my doll's house
yesterday. Perhaps . . .

No. That wasn't a good idea.

I looked for something else in one of the
drawers under the bench.

No. I didn't think these were going to be much help.

But there was something else at the bottom
of the drawer. I tugged hard at whatever it was.

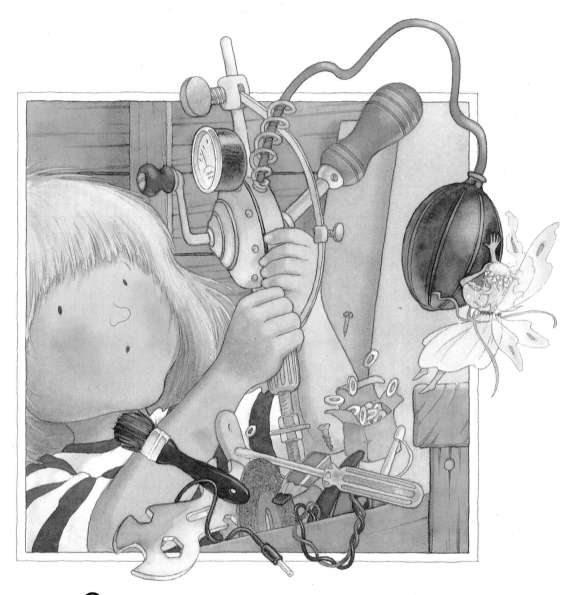

Oops! Whatever it was jerked out of the
drawer and knocked the poor fairy off the bench.

The fairy wasn't hurt. Just a bit dizzy.
She felt lovely in my hand as I picked her up
and put her back on the bench.

We were both fed up. We couldn't think
what to do.

Then I had an idea. Yes! A brilliant idea!

I ran back to the house as fast as I could.
The rain was still pouring down.

I had to get something from the desk in the
sitting room.

I was glad there was no one around. I didn't want anyone to see me. They might start asking awkward questions.

I ran back down the path to the shed.
My hair was soaked.

"This will do the trick!" I told the fairy and I
showed her a big roll of Sellotape.

I told her to keep very still. Carefully I bit off a little piece of Sellotape and stuck it over the tear in her wing.

There! It worked! The fairy was delighted.
The wing looked as good as new.

But would she be able to fly again? There was only one way to find out . . .

Yes, she could fly! Hooray! She flew around
the light three times and then floated back down
to the bench.

The fairy was very happy. And so was I.
And it had stopped raining.

We crept out of the shed. It was very bright outside. The sun had come out again and the path was steaming in the sunshine.

It was time to say goodbye. The fairy floated
gently up into the sky. "Goodbye fairy," I called.
"I hope I'll see you again."

I really, really do . . .